This book belongs to:

_____

_____

To Julia and
Paul, fellow billy
goats . . . and to Mom, for
playing the best troll who lived
under the bridge at Umstead Park ~ M. A.

For Caleb *x*
~ K. P.

tiger tales
5 River Road, Suite 128, Wilton, CT 06897
Published in the United States 2015
Originally published in Great Britain 2014
by Little Tiger Press

Text copyright © 2014 Little Tiger Press
Illustrations copyright © 2014 Kate Pankhurst

ISBN-13: 978-1-58925-459-6
ISBN-10: 1-58925-459-7
Printed in China
LTP/1400/1058/0914
10 9 8 7 6 5 4 3 2 1

For more insight and activities,
visit us at www.tigertalesbooks.com

The Three Billy Goats Gruff

adapted *by* Mara Alperin

Illustrated by Kate Pankhurst

tiger tales

High in the mountains lived three billy goats. They were called Baby Gruff, Middle Gruff, and Big Gruff.

All winter long an icy wind blew, and the
billy goats ate only dry thistles and scraggly,
thorny bushes. When at last the snow melted,
they set off for the valley below.

Down the mountain they trotted, **trip-trap! trip-trap!** to the old stone bridge. There, on the other side of the river, was the freshest, greenest grass they had ever seen.

Look at that yummy grass!

And so the billy goats lined up to cross the bridge — first Baby Gruff, then Middle Gruff, then Big Gruff.

But under the bridge, hiding in the shadows, was a BIG, ugly troll!

He had a **terrible** warty face.

He had **horrible** pointy ears.

RIVER RECIPES FOR TROLLS

He had awful, **stinky** breath.

And he liked to eat **anyone** who crossed his bridge!

So when Baby Gruff skipped
across the bridge with a
trip-trap! trip-trap! . . .

. . . the troll sprang up
from below, snarling
and slobbering.

"It's me," Baby Gruff squealed. "The littlest billy goat! I'm going to the meadow to nibble all the flowers."

"Oh, no, you're not!" roared the troll. "This is MY bridge. And I'm going to eat you up for breakfast, with some freshly buttered toast!"

Baby Gruff trembled. "Please don't eat me!" he squeaked. "I'm so little, you wouldn't even taste me! Wait for my older brother, Middle Gruff. He's bigger and *much* tastier."

The troll licked his lips. "Bigger? Tastier?" he cried. "Then I'll eat him instead. Now BE GONE WITH YOU!"

And so Baby Gruff
scurried over the bridge.

Trip-trap!
Trip-trap!

"Silly old troll," he giggled.

Soon after, Middle Gruff clattered across the old stone bridge, **trippity-trap! trippity-trap!**

The troll leaped up once more, growling . . .

Who's that trip-trapping

over **my** bridge?

"It's me," Middle Gruff bleated. "The next billy goat! I'm going to the meadow to munch all the grass."

"Oh, no, you're not!" roared the troll. "I'm going to gobble you up for breakfast, with a nice glass of milk!"

"Don't be silly," cried Middle Gruff. "I'm so bony, I'd make your teeth fall out. Wait for my older brother, Big Gruff. He's fatter and *much* yummier."

The troll started to drool. "Fatter? Yummier?" he shouted. "Then I'll eat him instead."

Now BE GONE WITH YOU!

And so Middle Gruff trotted
across the bridge.

Trippity-trap!

Trippity-trap!

"Silly old troll!" he snickered.

Finally, Big Gruff thundered up to the bridge.

"RAARGH!" roared the troll.
"Who's that trip-trapping over my bridge?"

He was very, VERY hungry by now!

Big Gruff stomped his hooves.
"It's me," he grunted. "The
biggest billy goat."

The troll's tummy was
rumbling and grumbling.
Up he jumped, bellowing . . .

And he knocked the troll right into the rushing river!

SPLASH!

"AARRGHH!"

howled the troll as the river swept him far away.

And so Big Gruff thudded over the bridge to join his brothers in the meadow.

TRIP!

TRAP!

TROMP!

"Silly old troll," he chuckled.

All summer long, the three billy goats Gruff crunched and munched the delicious green grass until they could eat no more. And they never, ever saw that **silly** old troll again!